A Bear Named Howard

Laurie MacKechnie

A Bear Named Howard
Copyright © 2015 Laurie MacKechnie
Rivershore Books
All rights reserved.
ISBN-10: 0692554939
ISBN-13: 978-0692554937

Dedication

To Candi, my angel friend, who made sure
that Howard came home.

Also, to The Big Brown One who galumphed
beside me on this journey.

Acknowledgements

First and foremost, I want to thank my husband, Mac, for being my chief editor, revision expert, cheerleader, and best friend. I also want to thank my dear friends, Marlene, Linda, Sue, and Nancy for their suggestions and encouragement throughout the writing of this book.

Prologue

The first one I saw upon my return was the ghost. The Colonel was confused about many things regarding the present time, but he understood love. His smile conveyed his pleasure at seeing me once again. My return answered many questions regarding all those who had disappeared over the years . . . never to return until today.

Let me tell you my amazing story!

My name is Walter, but it was changed to Howard on a fateful day a few months ago. In The Big White House, as we lovingly called our home, Howard was a name to fear and dread. You see, I am not the first Howard and I will not be the last. When you are given that name, it means you are taken from the home and friends you have grown to love, leaving them forever . . . until my return.

Perhaps I better start at the beginning, before I even had a name . . .

The Big White House

Chapter One
New Home . . . New Hope

"Hope starts as a tiny flame in the heart and either grows into a blaze or diminishes into embers."
Walter the Bear

It was a cold day in Minnesota and I was in an antique store watching customers mill about. I had lived on my shelf until my brown fur, and heart, had grown dusty with time. Many people had walked by the booth commenting on this or that saying, "My grandma had one of those," or "I didn't know that was an antique!" Nobody glanced my way . . . until that fateful day that would change my life. A woman walked by my shelf and her glance rested on me. As our eyes met, she stopped with a smile on her face and lifted me down into her arms. She blew the dust off my head and said, "Well, hello little guy! I think you need to come home with me!" I didn't know what to do! I wanted to scream, cry, and cheer all in the same moment. Instead, I pretended that I was stuffed from head to toe with cotton and that my heart wasn't beating a mile a minute!

The owner of the store walked up to us and inquired whether or not The Lady wanted her to take me up to the front desk while she shopped. She said, "No, thank you. I think I will keep him with me." For the first time in years, I remembered the warmth of being held close and the hope that life was being renewed for this old teddy bear.

Many years ago I had been bought as a birthday gift for a young child who had far too many toys. As she opened the box, a look of delight appeared on her face, but that was soon replaced with darting glances searching for more presents and bigger surprises. I was placed in the nursery on top of a dresser until one day when the maid picked me up to dust. Instead of putting me back, she threw me into a nearby toy chest. As the child grew, toys from the box were donated or sent to THE GARBAGE. I was fortunate enough to be dropped off at a second-hand store where I was purchased and took my place on the antique store shelf. That is where I sat until The

Lady glanced my way and our eyes locked. I had yet to learn the meaning of the word "love."

After a bit of shopping with me nestled in her arms, The Lady gave the owner of the antique store some money and we walked out of that musty old place for good! Air! I had forgotten the smell of fresh air and the feeling of a breeze rustling my brown fur. I had to control myself or my nose would start twitching! She tucked me in the backseat of her car, on top of her purse where I could see out the window, and we started for our destination: The Big White House.

The Big White House sat on a hill and was the largest home I had ever seen! My eyes were glowing with hope and anticipation and I had to quickly blink so that the tear in my eye wouldn't fall down my furry cheek and give me away. We drove by the stone wall surrounding the home and pulled into the driveway with the car stopping by the back door. The Lady gently picked me up and we climbed the stairs into the house. Little did I know how much my life would change as I was carried through that door!

Keeper of the Dreams

Chapter Two

The Residents of the First Floor

"Wisdom comes from years of experience,
piled onto understanding and compassion.
Without compassion, there is no real
wisdom."
The Giraffe

As we opened the entry door into the kitchen, we were greeted by a host of residents! The Lady only noticed the two dogs, but I was aware of so much more!

Let me tell you about the dogs first. Normally, I am frightened of big animals (something about "chew toys," stuffing, and slobber), but these two seemed interested only in sniffing me while barking a welcome. The Big Brown One, Arthur, appeared to be the sweeter of the two. Oreo, the black and white dog, was barking up a storm and seemed to be everywhere at once! The Lady petted them and scratched them behind their ears until they settled down. The dogs both circled a few times and curled up next to each other with their tails still wagging.

The other residents were what interested me more than the pets. First of all, there was another teddy bear at the entrance sitting on an old radiator. He seemed very interested in my arrival and sounded some kind of alarm to others deep within the house. I could see bears in adjoining rooms with keen eyes focused on me from all directions. However, the most amazing resident stood right in front of the woman, but only had eyes for me. I would learn later that he could not be seen or heard by humans because they just don't take the time to listen and really SEE.

He cleared his throat and, as he floated toward me, he said, "Hmm, Hmm . . . a new soldier to train in!" The Lady didn't even see him as he drifted right in front of her face, but I sure did! He introduced himself by saying, "I am Colonel Giddings and I have been in charge of the new recruits for as long as I can remember. Years ago, I lived here with my wife and child, but now I watch over the family who calls this house their home. You see, I passed on in the early 1900s and now protect the house, keeping everything and everyone in order."

I would eventually learn that The Colonel had lost his wife and newborn baby a day apart. After living with a broken heart for a number of years, when his time came, he felt the need to stay on in the house and keep everyone safe throughout the years . . . especially little children.

The Lady greeted her husband and gave The Man a kiss on the cheek. Then, she walked through a door and placed me on the dining room table, leaving the room to hang her coat in the front hall closet. I could tell that she had moved further into the house by the voices deep in conversation in a distant room. That was when I got some answers . . . and had more questions! The dining room was full of teddy bears and one giant stuffed giraffe!

The Giraffe was the one who addressed me first. In a voice both musical and comforting, she said, "Welcome, Small Bear. You have arrived at The Big White House and we are glad to welcome you into our family. When we get the chance we shall have a visit and learn more about you." She had the sweetest face I had ever seen and her sincerity made me feel at peace in my new surroundings.

The other bears in the room quietly called out to me in welcome as well. There was one in particular that would become a big part of my life. A little bear was sitting behind me on the table. She sang out, "My name is Ivy and I am pleased to see such a handsome teddy bear enter our realm. You are going to need a name. Let's see . . . you shall be called Walter." I turned to see where that beautiful voice came from and was immediately smitten! There sat the most adorable, white teddy bear I had ever seen!

The Giraffe gave her blessings to my new name and I thanked Ivy saying, "Walter is a name I will honor and cherish. I have never had a name before!"

The Colonel floated in silently and said, "Walter? Well, well . . . that is a respectable name for a young bear." I felt like I was finally home! The Giraffe, Colonel Giddings, and Ivy made me feel like I belonged. My heart just kept getting warmer and warmer as everyone made me feel like I was a part of something wonderful.

"I suppose you would like to meet the other inhabitants of the dining room before we move on. I will let The Giraffe do the introductions," said The Colonel. As The Giraffe looked around the room, her loving gaze landed on a fuzzy brown bear with his arm around a box with the label "Wish it! Dream it! Do it!"

"This," said The Giraffe, "is The Keeper of the Dreams. He records the special happenings for each bear at The Big White House and files them in the box. Your name, Walter, will be added today. Who knows where your story might lead?" Even though I could not see his eyes, I sensed a peaceful nature in The Keeper as he nodded in my direction.

The Giraffe asked me to share my deepest hopes and dreams with The Keeper. I blurted out, "I just want to make this world a better place!" The Keeper of the Dreams wrote my words on a card and placed it in the box. The Giraffe smiled all the way to her big brown eyes as she said, "Well, Walter, that is a noble goal. Somehow, I believe you will reach that dream."

I did not realize it at the time, but The Keeper of the Dreams had an index card for every bear that entered the house. The Keeper recorded life events for each bear, including experiences, dreams, and friendships. I would learn that many of the cards ended abruptly and only had a question mark as the last entry.

Next, my attention was drawn to a bear sitting up on the china cabinet. I learned that this bear, in a gorgeous, green velvet dress,

was Stella. Her job was to give advice on etiquette . . . whether you wanted it or not! I
discovered this when she looked down at me
and voiced her opinion of my manners. "I am
waiting for you to extend your paw and in-
troduce yourself," she said in a rather snooty
voice. "The newest member entering a group
of established bears should always offer their
information first!" I would have blushed if
that were possible for a stuffed animal. I hurriedly offered my name and a brief history of
where I had come from. This seemed to ap-
pease Stella as she nodded and moved a paw
like a queen waving at her subject. Hmmm . . .
I would have to watch my Ps and Qs around
that bear!

There were two more bears to be introduced and their appearance set me at ease
right away. The girl bear wore a cheerleading
dress while the boy bear behind her had on
a letter jacket from the same school. The Giraffe introduced them as Donna and Jim. They
were brought to The Big White House in hon-
or of The Lady's mother and father, whom
she had loved deeply. They had attended high
school together, fell in love, and brought The
Lady here when she was first born. I learned
that The Lady was the third generation of the

same family who had lived in this home. Her grandparents had actually bought the house from The Colonel! Jim and Donna just made me smile!

All of a sudden The Colonel said, "I will now take him on a tour of the rest of the house and assign him his duties. We run a tight ship here, Walter!" He bowed to The Giraffe before summoning me. "Follow me," he ordered. I replied, "Yes, Sir!" and fell into step right behind this stately apparition. As we left the dining room, there was a chorus of "Goodbyes" and "See you later, Walter!" Even Stella nodded her head and called, "Tah tah, Walter."

The Colonel picked me up and we floated toward the next room. From the dining room, we went through French doors into the front hall. It was a very elegant room with a grand piano, a lighthouse, and a hat tree. I was excited to see the piano because I LOVE music, but the lighthouse confused me greatly. When I asked about it, The Colonel explained, "The Man of the house loves lighthouses! The Lady bought him this one; it is about 7 feet tall. He wanted to put it outside, but she convinced him to place it here. On stormy nights, they turn it on as a beacon of safe travels to motorists passing by. By the way, the hall tree displays my top hat. When I had this house turned to face the pond back in 1905, I told them to make the new stairway into the basement tall enough so that I could wear my top hat and successfully descend the stairs without it touching the ceiling!"

"How did you turn the house?" I asked in awe.

"I used jacks and pulleys to lift it up off the ground. Then, using horses to turn the house 45 degrees, a basement was dug out and the house was lowered onto a new foundation facing the pond. I used to pay the men out front in military style. They would line up and I would sit behind a table and give them their money. Those were the days!" The Colonel proudly stated. I decided that this was a VERY interesting house!

In the front hall, sitting near the big door to the outside world, there sat a very prim and proper bear hugging an antique clock. This was The Time Keeper and she came all the way from Rye, England. When she was introduced, she explained her role in the house with the most wonderful British accent! "Welcome, Walter! I keep this beautiful clock running and let the bears know what time it is if they should ask. I also send warnings when it is close to the time The Lady and The Man return from work." I told her I was so glad to meet her and that I would try to visit her soon to learn about England! Then The Colonel set me on the floor and beckoned me to follow him.

We walked into the living room and I met The Love Bears. They were the two biggest stuffed animals I had ever seen and they sat in a chair, cuddled together by the fireplace. The look of love on their faces took my breath away. They both greeted me and smiled with genuine kindness. The Colonel introduced the pair, saying they would be there if I ever felt unloved or frightened. They also kept their eyes on the front hall and sounded the alarm if anyone walked through the door. From their vantage point, they could see any visitor arriving from the front of the house. Then they could alert the bears both upstairs and downstairs. "Time is of the essence when there is an intrusion," stated The Colonel. "We must be alert and prepared at all times!"

By this time, I had taken my eyes off The Love Bears and stood in awe as I turned around and saw books lining every wall! The entire room was surrounded with bookcases that were filled with old books! The Colonel told me that, in his day, there were no electronic entertainment devices. He found escape and enjoyment in books. "These were all collected by me back at the turn of the century. There are 2,544 editions in this library and I have read them all!" The Colonel remarked, with pride and warmth in his voice.

There were overstuffed chairs with a multitude of pillows, a fireplace, pictures of children . . . and bears! There were bears on the bookcases, bears on the furniture, bears in birdcages, bears EVERYWHERE! The bears all shouted out a hello to me and made me feel welcome. I thought that The Lady would certainly hear the commotion and come running, but Colonel Giddings explained that the humans in the house never heard any of the troops. Either they couldn't, or they didn't try hard enough.

In the midst of all of these books sat a very wise bear with glasses perched on the end of his nose. He was introduced to me as Library Bear. If I should ever need any information, I only need ask this knowledgeable fellow and he would get my answer in a short time! That might come in handy as I tried to figure out what I had missed, sitting on that dusty old shelf in the antique store for years! There were other bears in this huge room, but they would have to wait to be introduced another day.

I then followed The Colonel into the next room and saw even more bears! There must have been twenty new friends on the old radiator that heated the room and one friendly bear even riding on a rocking horse. They all greeted me warmly and I started to feel like this was going to be a wonderful place to spend my days.

The Colonel motioned for me to follow as we approached some steps leading upwards. It was a long winding staircase and I stayed close because I didn't want to lose The Colonel.

Brownie

Chapter Three

The Upstairs Residents

"Love is a gift that, once opened, must be returned."
Brownie the Stuffed Dog

The stairway was majestic! On the first landing, The Colonel stopped and looked up at a huge, white bear leaning over the banister. This bear waved a paw and beckoned me to move on up the stairs. The Colonel told me this bear was The Keeper of the Stairs. That meant that she knew all of the comings and goings of the family and could alert the bears of the approach of a human. He whispered to me that she might sometimes be misinformed and jump to conclusions.

We continued up the stairway to another landing where a large bear sat in a rocking chair. The Colonel smiled at the bear and spoke gently, "This bear was mine and I still sit with her in the rocking chair from time to time, when my duties allow." We moved up another short set of steps to the left and I was in the UPSTAIRS. This is where the family slept and I found it to be warm and inviting.

Our first stop was in the children's room, where The Lady's daughters had slept years ago. This is where I met The Jury! Near the ceiling, around the entire room, was a shelf with hundreds of teddy bears! I couldn't believe my eyes, but they all seemed to be welcoming . . . although they looked a bit stern. Evidently, they would judge a teddy bear if the bear broke one of the rules set forth by The Colonel. I didn't want to think about that yet, but I would certainly listen to The Colonel when he told me "The Rules of the House" and what my duties would be. I would find out much later that trials never took place because all of the bears did whatever The Colonel asked of them.

Next we went into the Reading Room, which had a magnificent view of the pond. I knew I would grow to love this room. Here, The Colonel explained, The Lady and The Man would sit in comfortable rocking chairs, sharing books and stories with each other. Years before, it had been the bedroom of The Lady's son. I could still feel the warmth and love that he had left behind after he grew up. This was going to be my room, as I would find out very soon.

Our final stop was the master bedroom. It was a huge room with a small living area near the front bay window. What caught my breath were the bears on the bed! There must have been fifteen or more and they all looked SO LOVED! Each one was worn and a bit tattered. They had an essence of peace and empathy about them and I wondered what they had been through to be placed in such a display of honor. I could hardly wait to hear their stories!

I was introduced to a few of The Bed Bears. First, there was Mr. Bear, who had belonged to The Lady's son when he was a little boy. Mr. Bear was adored by The Boy and went with him everywhere. He rode in the car, flew on airplanes, and even went to the family's cabin! He was so loved! I asked him how he had made it to this place of honor. He answered, "One day, when the little boy was about nine, he walked into the bedroom holding me tightly and asked his mother if she could take care of me. He was getting too old for a teddy bear, but he wanted to know that I would be safe. The mother took me into her arms and kissed my boy on the head. She then kissed my head and said that she would kiss me every day and think of her son. She told him I would be safe and cherished forever. She has kept her promise. Now and then, all of these years later, The Boy arrives home from college and comes up to check on me, giving my paw a gentle squeeze."

There was a bear wearing a Texas Christian University shirt. The Lady had taught school and Mickey, the TCU Bear, would visit one of her students' homes every weekend. Mickey would return each Monday to share his stories with the classroom of children. Of course, the weekly host would have to do the writing in Mickey's journal, but the class knew they were the words and memories of the bear. He had so many stories ranging from exciting to fascinating to heartbreaking. I would love to sit and hear some of his tales!

There was a white bear with "I love you" written in pink letters all over her fur. She was a gift from The Boy's twin sister. Another bear, with a beautiful red bow, had been a gift to The Lady from The Man. A fourth bear came all the way from California where he had lived at a bed and breakfast in Santa Monica. The many bears in that beautiful, old B & B on the west coast lived there in memory of a beloved owner. After The Lady purchased him from the establishment, he traveled with her to his new home in Minnesota.

All of the bears had been the recipients of many hugs, tears, and love. Some of their ears were almost loved off and they were so threadbare that their stuffing showed in a few places. I knew that their stories were all rich and meaningful and I could sense that these bears had earned their right to sit enthroned on the bed. It would be an honor to have a job where I could protect them.

Next, my eyes rested on a stuffed dog snuggled into the bears! What was HE doing there? When I whispered that question to The Colonel, he smiled and told me, "This is Brownie. He is perhaps the most beloved of all. The Lady received him as a birthday present when she was two years old and he has never left her. The Lady's mother, Donna, had to sew a turtleneck shirt around his body because The Lady had squeezed him so tightly through the years that his fur had worn right off! He also had the remnants of Tigress Perfume on his head where The Lady's mother would spray some cologne before she left for an evening out so that her little girl would feel safe and know her mother would always return.

That little dog had tearstains from sad times, sewn-on ears from when they had been loved right off, and hardly any fuzz left on his body. I could only hope to be loved that much someday! I bowed and told Brownie it was an honor to meet someone so very loved. Even though he didn't speak teddy bear, he smiled at me with a mouth that was crooked and almost worn off. His sewn-on eyes would melt the heart of any animal, stuffed or human.

Strangest of all, there was an antique cane nestled in amongst the stuffed animals on the bed! I just had to ask The Colonel about that!

"Friend Cane," The Colonel began, "belonged to The Lady's older daughter. Although the child liked a number of stuffed animals, she loved that old cane. She would carry it around with her and The Lady would extract Friend Cane from her daughter's sleepy grasp when she tucked her in at night. As the years passed, the daughter outgrew Friend Cane.

"One day, The Lady gently placed it on the bed with the rest of The Bed Bears and lovingly touched the wood saying, 'You have been deeply loved, Friend Cane, and you deserve a place of honor on The Bed.' Even though he rests on the pillows without moving, we all know that he is one of us and we honor him."

I knew the other special Loved Bears on the bed had amazing stories, but my attention was drawn to the rest of the room. There were more bears on the fireplace, dressers, chairs . . . everywhere I looked. I started to wonder if this was Bear Heaven, but then The Colonel told me about the "Howards" of the house.

Mickey

Chapter Four
The Warning

"You must earn the right to be loved. It is not a gift given without selfless acts and true commitment."
Misty Bear

"You will dwell with us in harmony and peace, but I must warn you of a possible threat," said The Colonel. "About once every week or so, The Lady walks through the house, selects a bear, and names it Howard. Then that bear leaves with her and is never seen again!" The other bears nodded solemnly and some even shivered in fear. As The Colonel held me at attention in his arms, a few bears chose to share memories about the loss of a friend who was given the name "Howard" and how they missed that bear each and every day!

One Bedroom Bear spoke of sitting in the big bay window, hoping against hope that his best buddy would one day return. Another little guy said he could still hear the cries of his friend as The Lady walked down the stairs with Beth dangling from her arm. Each one had been given the name Howard as she picked them up and whisked them away!

The saddest story of all was from Mickey. Although he was a Loved Bear and had earned the honor of residing on The Bed, he had lost a very special friend. For a few weeks, every time The Bed was made in the morning, one extra little bear was placed on The Bed by mistake. This teddy bear was named Misty and she felt so fortunate to have landed on The Bed. Misty even began to believe that she had done something in her life to give her the right to be a Loved Bear. She had become great friends with Mickey and was very attached to him.

The Lady had come to change her shoes and looked at the chosen ones propped up on the pillows. As she gazed at The Loved Bears snuggled together on the bed, she noticed Misty and said, "Where did YOU come from, little bear?" She picked her up and after a moment said, "You are my Howard today!" Misty cried and reached her furry little arms out to Mickey as she was carried through the bedroom door. Mickey tried to save her but couldn't reach her. All of the other bears called messages of encouragement to her as she passed them.

In the commotion, The Keeper of the Stairs became confused and sounded a warning of humans coming UP the stairs! That silenced The Jury who would have otherwise wished her safe, honest travels.

The Time Keeper told Misty, "Time will heal your sadness!"

The Library Bear called out, "Try to journal about your experience and send it to us. I will place it among the many volumes here in the library!"

Stella reminded her, "Use your very best manners even though it might be difficult!"

The Giraffe gently encouraged her with, "Take heart, Misty. We will all keep you in our thoughts."

Even The Colonel floated by to say, "Be strong and brave, Misty! At least that will help you as you head into this unknown battle!"

Mickey could hear her sobbing through the house until the back door shut firmly. Nobody ever saw her again and Mickey's heart remained heavy.

I listened to these heart-wrenching stories and remembered the dire prediction of possible events to come. However, with so many bears to choose from, why would I be singled out to leave? I tucked this story away in my fluffy head and decided it wasn't ever going to affect me!

The Love Bears

Chapter Five
My First Howard Experience

"Fear is the absence of knowing what is
ahead of you on your journey."
A Bear Named Howard

All of a sudden, there was some kind of alarm sounded from The Love Bears and then The Keeper of the Stairs echoed the warning. The Colonel put me down in the Reading Room just in time for The Lady to walk in the door. She stopped, scanning the room, and her eyes rested on me. My heart almost jumped out of my furry chest! Not only was I frightened for myself, but she had Ivy in her arms! "How on earth did you get up here, little guy? I thought I had put you on the dining room table! My mind must have been somewhere else! Let's put you on this rocking chair for now next to this little white bear I found in the dining room."

The moment she had appeared in the Reading Room, all of the bears took on a glazed look and froze in their places. Come to think of it, I had heard a small tapping sound right before she appeared. I realized that there was a code the bears used for alarms. I would need to learn that code and be more aware of my surroundings!

As she placed me on the rocking chair with Ivy, she looked up on a shelf and eyed a lovely teddy bear named Molly who had a big blue bow around her neck. She took her down from her perch and gazed into her face. "Hmmmm," The Lady mused, "you will make just the right Howard!" The teddy bear was tucked under The Lady's arm and whisked away, with fear written all over her furry face! There was the sound of soft whimpering from the little bear with the blue bow, but The Lady did not seem to notice. The Colonel sadly shook his head. The Big Brown One looked on with an air of anticipation, sniffed around, and turned to follow his owner down the stairs. He seemed to be panting and drooling with excitement!

After they left, I asked a bear sitting on a pile of books what just happened. He replied that another Howard had been chosen and that we would not see that bear again. I couldn't tell whether he was more sad or frightened, but I was just plain scared! "Where does she take the bears named Howard?" I asked my new friend.

"Nobody knows," he answered warily. "They just walk out the door with The Lady and The Big Brown One and they never return!"

"The Big Brown One has a part in this?" I asked.

The bear jumped off his pile of books and described the scene for me. "The Lady puts a bright red cape on The Big Brown One (whose real name is Arthur). She grabs a bear and out the door they go! Nobody knows what The Big Brown One does to the teddy bear, but when they return, he is tired, thirsty, and minus one teddy bear! As soon as The Lady takes the red cape off, he curls up and falls asleep, clearly exhausted!"

At that point, I decided to be as invisible to The Lady as possible! I would also stay clear of The Big Brown One!

There was a commotion from downstairs and an alarm was thumped. I was told to freeze! The events of the downstairs were relayed through a chain of bears and we discovered that the frightened little bear was leaving with The Lady and The Big Brown One . . . and he was wearing his red cape! My heart ached for that little bear with the big blue bow. I could faintly hear Molly calling a choked farewell before the door slammed shut.

Molly and The Giraffe

Chapter Six

Walter Meets With The Giraffe

"Trust: When you trust someone, you know in your heart that they will always be there to support you. If someone trusts you, never betray them because you will lose that trust in an instant."
Ivy the Bear

When the coast was clear, I asked Ivy to follow me. We slid down the banister and quickly approached the dining room in the hope of seeking counsel from The Giraffe. We peered around the French doors and there she was. In a hushed, gentle tone, she asked us to step into the light.

The Giraffe was the most stunning stuffed animal I had ever seen! Not only was she tall, but her beautiful eyes and long eyelashes were mesmerizing. At first glance, you might even mistake her for a real giraffe! She exuded warmth and wisdom. I knew I could trust her.

"What can I help you with?" she encouraged us gently.

I told her how frightened we were about
Molly leaving with The Lady and Arthur in
his red cape. "Dear Giraffe," I whimpered,
"can you tell us anything about the Howards
of The Big White House?"

It seemed as if she had fallen asleep. She
closed her eyes and breathed deeply. Finally she said, "Walter, it is not my place to tell
you where The Lady goes with The Big Brown
One. I know as much as most of the bears that
live here. I have my ideas, but I cannot be cer-
tain. If anyone might know for sure, it would
be The Colonel. He seems to know everything. Once, when I asked The Colonel what
he knew about these disappearances, he told
me to not worry. There was a reason for the
bears to leave, but discipline in The Big White
House might fall apart if the true story became
known by the troop of bears living here."

Later that day, The Big Brown One returned with The Lady and came upstairs to
jump up on the bed. He "galumphed" down
and was snoring before The Lady came to re-
move the red cape. I could only imagine what
had become of the little white bear with the
blue bow! It was a sad evening and we all

seemed to be solitary and quiet with our own thoughts.

Great Friends

Chapter Seven
Ivy and Walter

"If you have a good friend . . . a great friend,
life is brighter, the journey richer, and the
load lighter. Why? It is because you see
through two sets of eyes, travel life's road
with memories shared, and carry the burdens
together."
Walter the Bear

As my days began to blur into one huge
canvas of love, happiness, and adventure, I finally felt I had found a true home. Ivy was a
huge part of that feeling. Gone were the feelings of loneliness and hopelessness that had
been my constant companions.

We would sit in the rocking chair and talk
about anything from the weather to The Bed
Bears' stories, to our pasts and futures. She
was my dearest friend, adventure buddy, and
confidant. We shared secrets, finished each
other's sentences, and dreamed of a wonder-

ful future together in The Big White House.

On rainy days, we would wait until the coast was clear and then slide down the banister to visit our friends downstairs. The Keeper of the Dreams would pull out a card and tell the story of a bear from The Big White House. Other times, Stella would give us lessons in etiquette. The Colonel would tell stories of heroic acts while The Giraffe looked on with admiration and affection. When we would get tired, The Love Bears would always be there to cuddle us for a quick snooze and The Time Keeper would alert us to the impending arrival of The Lady or The Man. Then we would scurry up the stairs, crawl up into our rocking chair, and simply be content to hold paws.

On sunny days, we would creep down the stairs and, when we were sure the coast was clear, sneak out the doggy door to sit in the sun by the gazebo. When neighbors would glance our way, we would freeze in place until their attention would be drawn to something more interesting. A knock on the window would alert us to start the journey back upstairs to our beloved rocking chair.

One day, Ivy asked, "Walter, what makes you happy?" I thought for a long moment, weighing many things that warmed my heart.

I looked at Ivy and said, "What makes me happy is having a friend like you." Ivy leaned her head on my shoulder and said, "I feel the same way. Thank you for being my best friend, Walter."

I never dreamed that I would have a friend like Ivy and always tried to treat her with respect and love. My hope was that I could make Ivy's days as wonderful as she made mine. Friends are true gifts in life.

Colonel Giddings

Chapter Eight
Life Goes On

"Be of service and make a difference . . . no matter how small. Without a job, you can lose your direction and meaning in life. Listen to those in charge!"
The Colonel

Life went on quite smoothly for some time after my arrival. Two more bears were chosen, given the name Howard, and then frantically left with The Big Brown One in his red cape, but I had not been singled out . . . yet. This gave me time to get to know my surroundings and meet the other stuffed animals living in The Big White House. Most of our visiting took place at night, but we could also meet when the humans left the house. We were always alerted when the car pulled up in the driveway or someone came to the door. The bears used a system of knocking on the walls. Two knocks meant that someone was entering the house. Three knocks meant they were on their way upstairs. Not only were signals relayed throughout the house by the bears, but Oreo would bark as if crazed! At least she didn't seem to like chewing on soft toys!

One day, not long after my arrival, The Colonel appeared at the door to the Reading Room. "Hello, Walter!" he said. "It is time for you to be trained-in properly and learn the rules and regulations of the house." He picked me up, but once again I felt no warmth from his hands. He was a ghost, after all, and I was amazed that I didn't just fall to the floor!

He took me into the master bedroom and put me on the bed to sit with the bears lucky enough to reside there. The Colonel told me that I would replace Rosie, the young bear with the huge yellow bow, who was whisked away from her post a few weeks ago. Rosie's job had been to alert The Bed Bears when anyone was approaching. I learned that I would be warned by The Keeper of the Stairs, who would have heard the alarm from the first floor bears . . . along with the franticly barking Oreo. Then I was to make a soft whistling noise, accompanied by a series of short knocks, so that The Bed Bears could place themselves back into order.

As I sat with this group of bears on the bed, The Colonel stepped back and walked over to gaze out of the bay windows, lost in his memories. He looked wistful and I wondered what his life had been like as master of this house. I could only imagine the order and rules he had deemed necessary to run his own small army of servants. It was said that when The Lady's grandparents had bought the house in 1938, each room had battleship gray linoleum and all of the windows were shuttered with khaki-colored draperies. In keeping with his personality, a colorful décor was not one of his passions.

Just then, the alarm sounded from below. Two knocks! The dogs were barking and the message was relayed that The Lady was home. She was calling to The Big Brown One and she had the red cape in her hands!

The fear was palpable. Tension was showing on the faces of the bears around me. I, of course, had no idea what I was really expected to do since I was sitting ON the bed instead of in my rocker in the Reading Room. It was my job to warn The Bed Bears but I could see they were quite aware of the alarm. The Colonel disappeared as I heard three knocks! I could hear footsteps on the stairs.

The Lady appeared in the doorway to the bedroom and looked right at me! As everyone held their breath, she mused, "How did you get in here, little fella? I thought I left you in the Reading Room." I thought my time had come, but she smiled and returned me to my room, placing me back on the rocking chair next to Ivy. She glanced around the room and her eyes rested on a beautiful gray bear with actual jointed arms and legs. She walked over and picked her up, saying, "I will take you this time."

The little bear looked terrified! The Big Brown One was barking on the second landing of the staircase and finally came trotting into the bedroom. He had a red cape tied around his neck and a wild look on his face! They left the room together with The Lady holding a fearful, crying bear and the dog panting behind in hot pursuit! A hush fell throughout the room. It was a sad day when we lost a fellow bear.

After a series of farewells throughout The Big White House, we all heard the door close as The Lady left. With a mixture of sadness and relief, we heard the all clear sounded from below. I let go of the breath I had been holding, then hopped to the bedroom and over to the bed with Ivy at my side. The Bed Bears were already whispering about the fate of the little gray bear as The Colonel reappeared. When asked his opinion, the ghost simply shook his head and looked sad.

"I wish I knew more about the outside world," offered The Boy's bear. Mr. Bear continued, "I did get to travel some, but I never saw anything that would enlighten these events!"

The rest of The Bed Bears agreed with a few nods of their furry heads. For the most part, these special bears had been purchased by one of the humans and brought directly to The Big White House where they were eventually placed on the bed.

I had a few guesses involving a dog park, The Brown One, and a terrified bear named Howard. I took Ivy's paw and we walked slowly back to our rocking chair in the Reading Room.

Ivy and Walter

Chapter Nine
No Surprises

"Count your blessings and be grateful for all you have. Try not to dwell on what you do not have."
Walter the Bear

The seasons passed and I fell into a routine of sorts. Whenever The Lady was away, I would hop off the rocking chair with Ivy at my side and join The Bed Bears to listen to their life stories, which were rich with love. Sometimes, we would choose to slide down the banister and visit the bears on the main floor. Ivy and I would always hope to catch a few precious moments with The Giraffe who would share her wisdom.

I was full of gratitude for my life at The Big White House. I would see many bears leave the house . . . never to return. I also noticed the love that seemed to flow between the humans and the dogs. There were family birthday parties with laughter, cake, and presents, Sunday night dinners, and holidays where the humans seemed to be so full of love. The idea of destroying a teddy bear did not fit with what I knew of them. The bears were dusted every so often and placed back into position with a gentle loving hand. It was all SO confusing!

As the days turned into weeks and then months, I discovered the true friendship of dear Ivy. Ivy was beautiful, smart, and caring. I felt so fortunate that fate had landed us both in the same rocking chair! We would hold paws when we were frightened, laugh at the antics of some of the bears throughout the house, and sit at The Giraffe's hooves as she imparted her wisdom to all. We built our friendship on trust, empathy, and true caring. She was always there for me and I tried to be there whenever she needed a friend.

Ivy and I would look out the window of the Reading Room and wonder at all the activity on the pond in front of The Big White House. Birds would land and swim around in lazy circles, soon returning to the air with graceful wings. Deer would materialize for a brief drink of water and then disappear as silently as they had arrived. Children would skip rocks from the shore and wade in the water on warm summer days. As we sat on the window seat looking out at the world, we would discuss anything and everything . . . especially news that came into the house with The Lady or The Man. As they discussed current events, we would almost always hold the same opinion as each other. Whenever a Howard would depart, we would hold paws until the coast was clear and dry each other's tears. A true friend is an amazing gift and I cherished her.

I tried my best to do a good job of warning The Bed Bears when a human approached and soon I became an accepted member of the bear community. I would visit with The Giraffe, ride around the house with The Colonel and chat with my fellow bears in the Reading Room. However, the best part of my days was the time spent with Ivy. What a lucky bear I was! I had a warm, safe home, a true best friend, and a good job that mattered. I was surrounded by my fellow bears and, best of all, I had Ivy. Days and months passed and life was good, without too many cares or scares, until one day . . .

Walter Saluting

Chapter Ten

It's All in the Name!

"Being brave is one of the hardest things to do! Bravery is only possible because you care about those around you more than you care about yourself."
Walter the Bear

The alarm was sounded that day by the downstairs bears and flowed up to the second floor. I heard the taps and knew I must perform my duties. I hurriedly warned The Bed Bears as I heard footsteps on the stairs. The Lady walked into the Reading Room and gazed at the many furry faces, all of which avoided any eye contact. Then, all of a sudden, her gaze rested on me. Ivy and I were holding paws so tightly and I could almost feel her heart beat in fast rhythm with my own! My own little heart beat furiously and skipped a beat when she approached and lifted me gently into her arms. "Well, little fellow, today is your big day!" she announced as she headed out of the room and down the stairs with me in her arms. "Just let me get my coat and Arthur and then we will be on our way."

Now, I am not a brave bear, but I knew I must behave in a brave manner to save my friends from a horrible experience. Ivy was sobbing and kept crying out that she would never forget me! I called back that she had made my life so very wonderful. I would always carry her in my heart.

Many of the bears seemed to be in a sort of sad, panicked state. The Jury called out to me and wished me luck. The Keeper of the Stairs gave me one last high-five while shaking her head. The Love Bears held each other tightly and gently said they would keep me in their hearts as The Time Keeper noted the time of departure with a tear in her eye. When we walked into the dining room, Stella reminded me to mind my manners no matter what. Donna and Jim cheered me on with sadness in their voices. The Keeper of the Dreams took my card out of his box and entered the date and time of my departure with a shaky paw. Somehow, I knew he added a question mark as the last entry on my card.

As The Lady paused to put on her coat, she

placed me on the table for a moment. The Giraffe took this opportunity to whisper, "Take heart, Walter. The Lady has so much love in her heart that I can't believe there is a plan to harm you in any way! I just know that this is not the end for you." Take heart? My heart was breaking. Still, as terrified as I really was, I waved to all of my friends and smiled so that they would not feel my fear and pain.

Just as The Lady finished buttoning her coat, Arthur ran into the room with his red cape and a look of hungry hopefulness on his face! I was doomed!

Finally, The Colonel made an appearance. He commanded, "Walter, do not lose faith. I believe I know where you are going. Chin up, Soldier!" He saluted in my direction and as I returned the salute he vanished.

The Lady walked through the room and picked me up while calling to The Big Brown One. "Let's go, Arthur! We have a big day ahead of us!" she said, smiling. Big day? What could that possibly mean? I tried to put on a brave face as I waved one final farewell to all of my friends. The three of us, human, dog, and bear, walked out the kitchen door, never to return . . . or so I thought!

Arthur jumped into the backseat of the car

as I was placed gently in the front seat next to The Lady. I couldn't see anything from my lowly spot, but my imagination seemed to have 20/20 vision! I could picture the approach to the dog park as we maneuvered right and left, stopped for traffic, and even honked at something in the road. The Big Brown One was leaning over the front seat panting and drooling on my head! I was heartbroken and terrified! I tried to hang on to The Colonel's parting words. The Lady turned on the radio and started to sing. Country and Western was not my favorite music, but it did seem to soothe my nerves a bit.

Sophie's House

Chapter Eleven

No Dog Park!

"Confusion seems to be a mixture of fear and lack of information. As more information is revealed, the fear recedes and a glimmer of understanding surfaces."
Walter/Howard the Bear

After what seemed like a lifetime, The Lady parked the car. She went around the back to get Arthur on a leash and then returned to pick me up. The Big Brown One, red cape blowing in the wind, looked excited and full of hope for an enjoyable time. I looked for a place where The Lady could toss toys and things to Arthur, but no dog park was in sight. Instead, we approached a beautiful home with red shutters and smoke billowing out of the chimney. The Lady rang the doorbell at the front of the house and waited for a LONG time before anyone came to the door.

Finally, the front door slowly opened and

there stood the last thing I expected to see this day. A small, thin little lady stood in the open doorway with the saddest smile I had ever seen! When she saw Arthur, she brightened up perceptibly and invited us into her home. I felt the first glimmer of hope in my heart.

The front room was darkened by closed drapes. There was a musty smell, as if fresh air was seldom a visitor to this place. There were no teddy bears or other stuffed animals to be seen as we entered, but what caught my eye was a very large cat that seemed to sidle into the room unnoticed. Suddenly, I wanted to hide behind Arthur for protection! This cat did not look pleased to see any of us! She hissed at Arthur and tried to scratch him with her paw! The little lady said, "Hush Selma! Mind your manners! Our visitors are guests in our home!" Selma looked on in disdain, but she didn't hiss anymore. I noticed that The Brown One kept one eye on her!

The little owner of the house walked ever so slowly to a couch covered with blankets, pillows, and books. The table in front of the couch was littered with bowls, glasses, magazines, and mail. The Lady walked toward the couch and sat in a nearby chair, asking, "How are you doing today, Sophie?"

After collapsing on the couch, the little lady simply smiled and said, "Better now that you and Arthur have stopped by to see me!" My heart seemed to break when I looked at her eyes . . . the eyes of kindness, sadness, and suffering. At this point, as if not to be forgotten, Selma jumped up on the back of the couch to position herself like a shawl on Sophie's shoulder.

The Lady said, "I brought you a little friend to keep you company! He is here to remind you that somebody cares!" The cat looked less than impressed, but the little lady's eyes welled up with tears as she reached out and took me into her arms.

Sophie gently hugged me and said, "Hello, little fellow. I hope you like to snuggle and take long naps. Life is not too exciting around here right now!" Suddenly, I was swept back in time and saw myself sitting on that shelf in the antique store. The memory of desolate feelings and loneliness overwhelmed me and I understood what I needed to do for this little lady. She needed a friend; I could be that friend. I melted into her arms as she held me close.

The cat jumped down onto Sophie's lap and gave me a perfunctory sniff. She then turned up her nose and jumped up on the arm of the couch where she planted her claws into the material, making some scratching noises. "Stop that, Selma! You will destroy my couch," Sophie said with little conviction. The cat glanced at her owner with a look of surprise that turned into one of adoration. I could tell she loved the little lady even though I bet she would deny it, if asked.

The Lady and Arthur were now in the kitchen where the dirty dishes from the table were already being placed in the dishwasher. As they came back into the room, my new human asked about my name. "His name is Howard," The Lady responded, with great respect. "He really is such a sweet guy and I knew that he would brighten your days."

So The Howards don't go to the dog park after all! The Lady takes them to people who need a little extra love and warmth. No wonder The Colonel refused to share his knowledge! The Bears at The Big White House would fuss and fight to leave with The Lady and a red-caped Arthur. All semblance of order would be lost! More than anything, The Colonel loved order!

After a short visit with a lunch provided by The Lady and a lot of fussing about the living room to make Sophie feel comfortable, it was time to go. Arthur, who had been scratched, petted, and rubbed, lifted his big graying head off of Sophie's lap and looked at The Lady expectantly. She was putting on her coat with promises to return very soon. Sophie waved from her chair as the pair opened the door to leave. Selma jumped up and took her rightful place on Sophie's lap.

At that moment, Arthur turned around and winked at me! I was SHOCKED! I am sure it was a real wink! His expression held a combination of wisdom, empathy, and affection. I started to wonder how much he knew about the teddy bears at The Big White House! Is it possible that he could hear and see everything we had been up to? The door closed after them and I was left behind with my musings.

Selma

Chapter Twelve

Being Howard

"When you mix understanding and affection it is easy to feel empathy. You can't simply look down at someone's shoes, but you must place your feet in those very shoes and walk their journey. Then, and only then, you can empathize and truly understand their challenges."
Walter/Howard the Bear

Sophie gave a big sigh and picked me up off the couch where I had been placed. "Well, here we are, Howard. Let's watch a bit of TV together and then take a nap."

She turned on the TV and sat me right beside her so that I could see the screen. My mind was racing! Arthur doesn't eat the Howards that have left with The Lady! I was proof of that! Where had they all gone then? When I got the chance, I would explore Sophie's house to see if any had ended up here. Somehow I had my doubts. In the meantime, I snuggled in close to Sophie and kept one eye on that cat!

I must have dozed off because I awoke to hear a soft snoring sound coming from Sophie. I wiggled out from beside her on the couch and silently slid to the floor. First, I checked the kitchen where I found no bears. Next, I went upstairs to the bedroom, but nobody was there either. Finally, I went down to the dining room where I did not find my lost friends, but I did find THE CAT!!!!! I was doomed!

"What are YOU snooping around for?" Selma asked in a hissing kind of voice. "I don't like change and especially something that sneaks around MY house! Now answer me if you like your stuffing on the inside of your furry little hide!"

I took a chance and hoped that she didn't really like to eat teddy bears. I had seen, however, what she had done to the couch! Perhaps flattery would work. "You are looking sleek and lovely today, Miss Cat," I responded with a slight tremble in my voice. "I was only looking for some of my friends who were taken from my home and brought . . . somewhere," I pleaded. "I know they are not here but can't stop looking for a sign that they might have been here and left."

If cats could laugh out loud, this one would have. She sauntered in my direction to stand over me while she hissed softly and said, "There are no teddy bears here! There never WERE any bears! EVER!!! You are the first and only bear to end up here! How do you like that?" At that, Selma stretched and showed off her claws and added a B-I-G yawn to display her set of curved, sharp teeth! Then she added with a venomous smile, "Furthermore . . . I've got my eyes on you!"

Well, that wasn't much of a welcome! At least she didn't eat me! At that moment, Sophie gave a little moan and opened her eyes. When they focused on me in the dining room, a smile spread across her face and she greeted me by name. "Hello, Howard! Did Selma carry you in there? I think it is time to try to eat a little supper. What do you think?" she asked as she sat up and stretched gingerly. I simply stared straight ahead as she picked me up and headed for the kitchen. The cat followed right at our heels.

Sophie rummaged through the cupboards and then focused on the refrigerator. She pulled out a container of soup that The Lady had left and warmed it up in the microwave. That cat followed her everywhere! When we finally settled down at the kitchen table with a few crackers to add to the soup, I found myself propped up on the table right in front of Sophie. She took a few spoonfuls and ate part of a cracker. Then Sophie shook her head and pushed her bowl away. She almost ate less than I eat! My heart started to ache for her and I felt the first stirrings of affection for this woman.

The phone rang and she slowly walked across the room to answer it. "Hello?" she said. I could hear the person's voice at the other end and it sounded concerned. Sophie replied, "I am feeling better than I did right after the chemotherapy. Don't worry about me! I am one tough old bird!" I felt my heart melt. Meanwhile, Selma saw her chance and finished off the soup and remaining crackers.

So, she has cancer! That would explain a lot. The puzzle pieces were beginning to fit together. The Lady from The Big White House had brought me to help Sophie feel better. I could certainly take on that job! When she returned to the table after her phone conversation, I tried to look sweet and then made myself topple over on the table. She smiled and said, "Did you eat too much, Howard? Let's go back on the couch and read some books."

We settled under a cozy blanket in the living room and she began to read aloud to me. The book was about a young woman who wanted to be a firefighter. She seemed to hit roadblocks at every turn. Finally, someone listened to her dream and allowed her to shadow the firefighters. It was a very exciting story as she rode along and even helped save a life! I wanted Sophie to read more, but I could tell she was getting tired.

"Just another little snooze, Howard. Then we can go sit outside and watch the sun set in the west." As she settled in, she hugged me tightly and allowed the cat to join us on the couch. What a strange trio we made! I still kept one eye on that Selma at all times!

Arthur
The Big Brown One

Chapter Thirteen
The Big Brown One Speaks!

"Do not have expectations for others'
behavior. When you least expect it, you will
be either disappointed or shocked!"
Arthur the Dog

The days rolled by and pretty soon a week
had passed. Our days took on an easy cadence
and I had been lulled into a calm schedule.
Then one day there was a knock on the door,
shattering our reverie, and in walked The Lady
with Arthur. After giving Sophie a warm hug,
The Lady started tidying up a bit. As she visited from her usual place on the couch, Sophie
asked The Lady, "Would you please bring me
that small box from the bookcase?" This gave
Arthur a moment to saunter over and stand
beside the table where I had been placed upon
their arrival. He stepped right over the cat who
took a swipe at one of his legs in a good-natured sort of way.

Arthur and I stared into each other's eyes for the longest moment and then, all of a sudden, HE SPOKE TO ME! It was hard to understand his growling speech, but I could make out most of it. "I informed The Giraffe as to your whereabouts and she sent you a message!" Arthur said. "She told me to tell you to remain strong and hopeful. She also said to try to be kind to the cat. I am not sure if that last bit was for you or for me."

"YOU CAN TALK!" I whispered. "Why wait until now to let me in on that little secret?"

He sniffed around the floor for crumbs and softly answered, "Why would I tell anyone? It seems that I wouldn't have to do that until someone really needed to know."

My fluffy head was shaking, but then I saw a chance to clear up some confusion. It was time to get some answers to my lingering questions. "How is everyone at The Big White House? Did The Giraffe tell the others where I am? How is Ivy? Can you tell her I am okay? Do I ever get to come home? Why do I have to be nice to that cat?"

Arthur snorted and said, "I have never heard so many questions from anyone! I do not know the answer to any of your questions, especially about being nice to the cat, but I will talk to The Giraffe when I get home. Perhaps I will have some answers next week when we visit."

Sophie and The Lady were finishing up with their visit, so I was afraid to make any more of a fuss. I was not sure how much we could get by with before they would notice our conversation. The Lady had brought a lunch and added some lemonade from the refrigerator. She gave Sophie another hug, said goodbye, and took Arthur with her out the door. I could hardly wait for their next visit!

The Memory Box

Chapter Fourteen

The Memory Box

"We cherish things only because they remind us of the people we love. Memories of loved ones fill the heart with peace and joy."
Sophie

Sophie came over and, with a gentle hand, picked me up from the kitchen table. I always felt my heart melt when she held me close in a loving embrace. As she walked across the room, I noticed that The Lady had placed a box on the table before she left with Arthur. Sophie sat down gingerly on the couch and pulled the box toward us. She looked me right in the eye and softly said, "Well, Howard, I want to show you what is in this Memory Box. It holds some of the things I value more than anything in this world! I have not shared these treasures with anyone before you."

I was honored beyond words and could only guess what was inside the beautiful box.

The Memory Box was painted a soft yellow with flowers added in reds, pinks, and blues. The box itself was a work of art. When she lifted the lid, I was mesmerized! Here are some of things I saw:

- A beautiful sapphire ring
- A well-worn dog collar
- A gold pocket watch
- An old dollar coin
- Pictures of a kind-looking gentleman
- Greeting cards
- A worn diary
- Newspaper clippings
- A beautiful bookmark
- A smooth stone
- Handwritten notes
- A dried rose
- Theater tickets
- A large shell
- An antique brooch

I looked up at Sophie and her eyes were misted over with tears. With a catch in her throat, she began . . .

"Let me tell you about my Memory Box, Howard. Everything I have placed in here has a beloved memory attached. The ring was a gift from my husband on our first wedding anniversary. This is him in the picture. Wasn't he handsome?

"The brooch was my mother's and the rose is from the last anniversary I shared with Frank, my husband. I lost him five years ago and miss him every single day.

"The dog collar was from my most beloved dog. Rosie lived to be 15 before she went to be with Frank. That's when I invited Selma to live with me.

"Everything in this box invites a treasured memory. That's why I call it my Memory Box. I add to it but never take anything away. Once a memory is cherished, it is always cherished."

We spent the better part of the afternoon looking through the box. Sophie held me in her lap as she traced her life's journey with the items in the box. She would gently pick up an item from the box and talk about the memories associated with the beloved item. I felt so privileged to have the chance to look into the Memory Box and share Sophie's treasures. I realized I knew her so much better now and my fondness grew to something even greater. I found that I cared deeply for Sophie.

Arthur
On the Job

76

Chapter Fifteen
A Conversation with Arthur

"Always choose kindness."
The Giraffe

During the week, Sophie would leave for a few hours and then return home looking tired and weak. She always gathered me into her arms and then would flop down on the couch for a nap or to watch TV. I could feel her ribs when she hugged me now. By this point, I cared for her deeply and worried she was not eating enough.

When The Lady arrived with Arthur at the end of the week, I waited until the humans started their visit and then tried to get Arthur's attention. "Psssst . . . Arthur!" I whispered. He looked at me and then pretended to be sniffing his way across the room to where I sat in an armchair. "What did you find out?" I asked.

"Not much," said Arthur. "The Giraffe

kindly refused to answer most of my questions, but she told me to keep your story to myself. Though, I don't think the other bears would listen to me even if I tried to tell them you were safe! They remain frightened of me and would only hear growling instead of words. The Giraffe is trying to figure it all out and will let me know when she has some answers."

At that moment, The Lady called Arthur over to her side so that he could spend some time with Sophie. You could tell that Arthur was the happiest dog on earth as Sophie rubbed his ears and spoke loving words to him! While the cat looked on in disdain, Arthur would put his paw up on Sophie's lap if she was not giving him enough attention and then nuzzle her arm if he needed his ears scratched again. What a life!

Before he left, I had one more request. "Arthur, can you come closer?" I asked. In reply, he snorted and shook himself as he walked nonchalantly across the room. When he got close enough, I told him my concerns about Sophie not eating enough. Could he somehow let The Lady know? Arthur told me he would try, but humans rarely listen. He would have to be creative!

With that, he walked into the kitchen and came back with a bag of cookies hanging from his large teeth. He gently placed them in The Lady's lap and then transferred them to Sophie's lap. The humans thought it was cute but did not understand the message. He returned to the kitchen and came back carrying a bag of bread. He placed this in Sophie's lap and then turned to look deeply into The Lady's eyes. As he did this, Sophie said, "Even though the bread and cookies look good, I don't have the strength to go out to the kitchen to make anything."

A look of comprehension passed between Arthur and The Lady as she said, "Why don't I make you a few sandwiches and bring a cooler out here with juice and treats? You could just reach inside the cooler to get whatever sounds good. I'll whip up a few more treats at home and bring them by next week." Sophie's eyes welled up with tears as she admitted that she would appreciate that very much! I could not believe that I once thought The Lady to be cruel and heartless. She was filled with kindness.

More appointments, more naps, a few visitors, and an attempt to eat a treat from the cooler. That is how our week passed. I noticed that Sophie never complained. I knew she felt

sick and that there were times when she felt a bit lost and lonely, but she would always give me a hug and say, "Aren't we lucky, Howard? We have so much to be thankful for!" What an amazing woman! My fondness grew into love.

Arthur

Chapter Sixteen

Still No Answers

"Secrets are hard to keep. One little slip and
the secret is now the news of the day."
The Giraffe

The next visit from Arthur and The Lady
made me smile! They entered and The Lady
was laughing! Arthur had a big bag hanging
from his mouth and headed right to Sophie!
The Lady said that when she got the red Therapy Dog bandana out and placed it around his
wide head, he ran over to grab a big bag of
fresh cookies she had just made. He would not
give it up, so The Lady said she asked him if
he wanted to take them to Sophie. In response,
Arthur had headed for the door with the bag
in his mouth and his big brown tail wagging
wildly! Sophie was delighted and ate two of
the chocolate chip cookies right there!

I could tell that The Lady was taking this
in and would probably bring cookies and oth-

er goodies each visit now. It also looked like she would be making a hot lunch for Sophie during their time together each week. Today's menu was spaghetti and meatballs. The Lady, whom I once feared, had turned out to be a loving, compassionate person. How could I have been so wrong?

Still no answers from The Giraffe! Why wouldn't she want Arthur to tell all of my friends that I was okay? It would erase their fear and give them hope! If my friends could only know that Arthur's red cape was a bandana signifying that he was a certified Therapy Dog! The Howards would be proud as they left with Arthur and The Lady to comfort people in need! I bet there had been a few more frightened Howards that had left The Big White House by now. They could have been spared the agony of leaving their friends and home for the unknown. Each Howard would know that they need not be afraid and were headed on a mission of mercy. However, The Giraffe always knew best! She must have had her reasons for keeping my whereabouts a secret. I would just have to be patient and have faith.

Chapter Seventeen

Emergency!

"When faced with the unexpected, take a deep breath and weigh the options. If nothing else, stand back and support The One who has a plan."
Arthur the Dog

As the weeks turned into months, our routine remained pretty much the same. Sophie would leave from time to time and return exhausted. I noticed that she was beginning to look gaunt and defeated as time went on. One day, I realized that Sophie was too weak to even lift her head! I was frantic! I attempted to get Selma's attention, but she was lying on the floor, warmed by a sunbeam and fast asleep. I even tried to tickle Sophie under her chin to make her move, but she just held me tighter! I could only let her hold me in her arms and pray for a miracle.

Suddenly, there was a knock at the door,

a pause, and then the sound of a key unlocking the door! Thank goodness that Sophie had given The Lady a key to the house in case she would need to enter for some reason. She walked through the door calling out to Sophie. The Lady looked very concerned as she looked at her friend and asked a few questions. Arthur had followed The Lady in and began licking Sophie's arm as he glanced at me in alarm. When Sophie couldn't get up with help, The Lady went to the phone and dialed three numbers, 9-1-1.

Pretty soon, I could hear sirens approaching! Suddenly the room was full of people, and everything was bigger than life! After trying to get Sophie to drink something, the people in uniforms put something over Sophie's mouth and nose to help her breathe. My world was crashing down all around me and my heart was beating right out of my furry little chest! To my surprise, Arthur gently picked me up with those huge teeth and moved away from the hubbub, plopping me down by a bookcase where he let me snuggle up close to his big chest. It was only a moment later that Selma quietly joined us, curling up within Arthur's big paws. Our hearts seemed to beat in a fast unison as we watched and waited.

Then, to my horror, they put Sophie on a rolling bed and started for the door! The Lady called out that she would take care of Selma. Suddenly, they stopped as Sophie murmured something through her mask. The Lady rushed back, snatched me up and shoved me into Sophie's arms. After that, The Lady swooped down and picked up Selma, grabbed Arthur's leash and we all went out to the ambulance together. Arthur was frantically panting and trying to say something I couldn't understand. The Lady waved goodbye and we zoomed off down the road. Even though I could be of little help on the trip to the hospital, I knew I could comfort her as I snuggled closer.

Those days in the hospital will always be a blur to me. There were tests, nurses, doctors, and more tests. Sophie slept a lot but kept me close to her at all times. The Lady and Arthur actually came up to the hospital each day to visit. Even though she was incredibly weak, Sophie was always glad to see them. I think the nurses and doctors liked seeing Arthur more than anyone! He would lean in on them and lick their hands while they would scratch his back and say how much this helped them feel calm. Arthur didn't have a chance to update me on anything. There were too many eyes!

Sophie's Front Porch

Chapter Eighteen

Home At Last!

"To understand deeply, you must listen . . .
really listen."
Walter/Howard the Bear

Finally, Sophie was well enough to go home! I felt like I was going home as well. The Lady came to the hospital to drive us to the house. Sophie needed a lot of help to make this journey because she was so weak. Finally, with The Lady supporting Sophie by the arm, we walked through the door of the little house where we were met by Selma. Evidently, The Lady had come over every day while we were gone to feed her and spend a bit of time with the cat. Selma said, "It's about time you got back! I have needs, you know!" she hissed at us. Even though the words were harsh and selfish, the look in Selma's eyes showed so much love and relief! She couldn't seem to stop rubbing up against Sophie's leg and even gave me a rough little lick with her tongue. The cat had a heart after all!

It felt so good to snuggle on the couch with Sophie and watch our favorite shows on TV again. She seemed to be feeling better and getting stronger. Arthur and The Lady would stop in every day, but there never seemed to be a chance to get any updates from The Big Brown One.

Then one day, Sophie felt so good that The Lady suggested that they go and sit out on the sunny front porch. She grabbed a shawl and they were on their way out the door before they gave any thought to a quiet dog or a silent bear. This was our chance to catch up!

Arthur sat down on the floor beside the couch. His big head had turned white with age over the years, but those brown eyes were still bright and intelligent. How could I have EVER been afraid of this gentle giant? I didn't want to waste any time, so I got right to the heart of the matter. "What have you found out from The Giraffe?" I asked in whispered tones.

Arthur sighed and answered, "Not much really. I can repeat what wisdom she felt she could share with me. This is what the big dog learned from The Giraffe . . .

"My dearest dog, we have lived in this

house for years together and I wish I had more answers to your questions." The Giraffe continued, "I do know that when the bears leave with The Lady, they are very frightened and sad. Knowing The Lady, it is my opinion that they come to no harm, but how can I prove that? None of them have returned to tell their story so, until that day, I remain in the dark.

"You tell me that Walter is safe and happy at another home. I am afraid that the bears would not believe this story coming from you. They fear you and do not seem to be able to trust my advice that would lead them to friendship with the dogs. Even The Colonel seems to remain indifferent or silent on this issue. At times, I feel he knows more than he lets on. When asked, he speaks in riddles about the bears that are taken away.

"If only one bear could return to us and tell their story, we could all live such different lives. Lives full of hope and anticipation for what might be ahead. I believe you, dear old Arthur, but I am afraid others would not."

With a huge sigh, The Big Brown One concluded with, "That is all I know, Walter. She has her reasons to keep your journey a secret. I do not question her wisdom. I would not like to question The Colonel either. Communication between us is seldom and brief. He is the Alpha in the home and we do as he commands. If he knows about you, he doesn't want the others to be informed at this time."

At this point, the two women returned from the porch with a gust of wind ushering them inside. The Lady said, "I hope you kept an eye on things in here, Arthur and Selma. We wouldn't want 'Howard' to disturb anything on the couch or get into trouble!" At this, they both laughed. The Lady gave Sophie a hug and said, "I am so glad that all of your medical tests turned out great! No more chemotherapy for you! Now you can think about getting stronger. Remember to get plenty of rest and eat those meals in the refrigerator! Arthur made sure I brought fresh cookies as well!"

The Big Brown One and I had a chance to share one last, affectionate glance before The Lady put his leash on and they headed toward the door. As they left, Arthur turned and winked at me. For the first time, I felt like a true and beloved friend was leaving and my heart was touched by that awareness.

The Letter to Sophie

Chapter Nineteen

Spring Brings Beauty

"Change is always a challenge. Even if it is a good change, it still takes time to embrace it and move forward. One has to come to terms with the new responsibilities involved."
The Colonel

As spring blossomed into summer, Sophie bloomed like the flowers in her garden. We would go outside and sit on the porch swing together where she would talk to me about her life. Selma would prowl around in the garden and roll in the grass. Sometimes, visitors or neighbors would stop to visit and I would simply sit in her lap and listen. One day, the mail carrier stopped by with a letter from her sister who lived in Florida. Before he walked away, he asked Sophie about me! "Why is that little fella always with you when I see you?"

Her answer surprised and humbled me when she said, "Howard was a gift from the therapy dog team that comes to visit me each week. He has seen me through the worst of my cancer journey and was always there when I needed a friend." The mailman smiled and whispered, "We all need friends like that, don't we?"

After he left, Sophie opened the letter from her sister and read it aloud to me. One paragraph talked about planning a visit to Florida when Sophie felt up to flying down there. She picked me up and actually looked me straight in the eye and said, "I do believe I will go in the fall. My only concern is what will happen to you and Selma when I go to Florida. Well, we have the summer to worry about that, don't we, Howard!"

Sophie's Garden

Chapter Twenty
Glorious Summer!

"It seems we need to go through bad times to truly appreciate the good times."
Sophie

That summer was the best time of my life! We spent long hours sitting on the porch, watching the sun set in the west. We listened to the birds singing and watched fluffy, white clouds drift by in a beautiful, blue sky. As her strength grew, Sophie spent time in the garden tending to her colorful, fragrant flowers as I watched from my perch on the lawn chair near the gate. She played the piano in the evenings as the curtains danced in the breeze, keeping time with the music. I got to hear that lovely voice as I sat on top of the piano, humming along quietly.

As the days grew shorter, I noticed a change in Sophie. She was stronger, happier, and more independent. She didn't carry me everywhere with her and sometimes I would sit for hours on the couch before she returned from some outing. I was thrilled that her health was returning, but I was lonely. She always took me to bed when it was time to sleep, but I wasn't hugged quite as tightly anymore. I wondered if I would soon be forgotten altogether.

Chapter Twenty-One
I AM STILL LOVED!

"Sometimes we are loved even when we feel
unlovable!"
Selma the Cat

Suddenly, it was autumn and the world took on a golden hue in the trees, the garden, and even in the air. As the days grew shorter and the temperatures cooled, Sophie began to prepare for the trip to visit her sister. As I was watching her pack for Florida, she suddenly turned toward the head of the bed where I sat among the pillows. Picking me up, she gently tried to squeeze me into her suitcase. When I didn't exactly fit, she softly whispered, "It might be time for you to help someone else who needs a friend; someone who can't face the day without your furry little face to get them out of bed. I will talk to my friend about that before I leave."

My little heart ached with love for this

woman and I held back a tear. I would miss Sophie, but maybe there was someone else who needed me more! Maybe, just maybe there were bigger things to come!

After Sophie fell asleep that night, I tip-toed into the living room. It was as if something was pulling me in that direction and I found myself in front of the Memory Box. As I reached over to lift the lid, I heard stealthy paws slowly approaching from the kitchen. Selma came right up to me and hissed, "What makes you think you can go into that box? It isn't your box!" I told her that I was probably leaving soon and I wanted to take one more look so I could remember Sophie even better.

As I lifted the lid, I caught my breath. There, lying right on top of the pile of treasures was a picture of ME! With trembling paws, I picked it up and held it close. I was loved and cherished and would remain in Sophie's memory forever! My heart grew about three sizes and a tear formed in my eye. I looked at Selma, and she had tears in her eyes as well. "Selma, why are you crying?" I asked.

She answered, "Nobody has ever loved me. I was abandoned as a kitten and showed up on Sophie's porch after a life of hunger and neglect. I grew to love her and hoped that she felt the same way. Now, she is leaving for Florida and I will be cast outside to fend for myself again."

I responded, "Selma, you ARE loved! I can see it in Sophie's eyes when she scratches your ears and cuddles you in her lap. She will make sure you are always loved and safe." I just knew that Sophie would take care of that cat! As I placed my picture back in the box, I disturbed a postcard and there below it, in all its glory, was a big picture of Selma! I called out to her and she came over to gaze in awe at the picture as her tears fell on other treasures.

"Well," sniffed Selma, "I guess she does love me! Who wouldn't?" Even though the words sounded snippy, her tone of voice gave her away. As she licked her paw and touched it to an ear, I could tell she was moved beyond measure.

Airport

Chapter Twenty-Two

Parting Is Such Sweet Sorrow!

"When you lose something or someone, you need to weigh the joy you felt before the loss against the pain you feel now. It is almost always worth the anguish."
Walter/Howard the Bear

The next morning, as I awoke from a restless night's sleep, I could tell something was different. There was a current in the air that made me uneasy. Sure enough, Sophie came into the bedroom, lifted me up, and looked directly into my eyes as she spoke. "Howard, I can't thank you enough for being my companion during this most difficult journey." There were tears in her eyes now. "I am getting a ride to the airport from The Lady and I will be leaving you with her when I go. My sister in Florida wants me to stay for the winter and I think it will be a bit warm for a bear like you," she shared, with a sad smile. "It would be selfish for me to take you along, but I want you to know how much I love you, Little Bear. There might be someone else who needs you more now."

Then Sophie turned to Selma. "I know you are not going to like this very much, Sweet Kitty, but you have to go in this crate. I am taking you to Florida with me and you can fly in the airplane right at my feet where I know you will be safe."

Selma looked at Sophie and then walked slowly over to me. She nuzzled my ears and whispered, "I will never forget you, Howard. You are a true friend." With that, she jumped off the bed and sauntered right into the traveling crate!

Sophie was shocked and said, "If I didn't know better, I would think you understood everything I just said!"

A car horn sounded and then there was a whirlwind of activity as suitcases were hurried out to the trunk and locks were checked on the house that had been my home for almost a year. Selma, in her carrier, was gently lifted into the backseat and Sophie held me in the car as we departed for the airport. I felt such a mixture of anticipation and sadness, all at the same time.

Finally, we arrived at the airport and Sophie stepped out of the car with me in her arms. She held me tightly and whispered in my ear, "I will love you always, Howard. Don't forget me. I will hold you in my heart forever." As she hugged The Lady goodbye, Sophie was crying and said, "Take good care of Howard for me. Remember what a special bear he is and always keep him safe." I could hear Selma's meow as she called out that I wasn't half bad and that she would actually miss me . . . a little. At that, Sophie handed me to The Lady, picked up Selma's carrier, and disappeared through the airport doors. My heart was breaking.

Ivy

Chapter Twenty-Three
What Will the Future Hold?

"A house is a place; a home is a feeling."
Walter/Howard the Bear

Back in the car, The Lady wiped a few tears, picked me up, and then looked directly at me before she started the engine. I looked right back into her eyes. In a voice full of emotion she almost whispered, "I do believe that there is more to you than just a fluffy head. Well done, Howard. Well done." She then tucked me in next to her purse on the front seat and we were off.

Off to where? Would I get another Sophie? Oh, how I wished Arthur were in the back-seat so that he could growl a bit of encouragement. I could only wait and trust The Lady. She had certainly made my life richer than before. Much like that first ride with The Lady so long ago, I could only sit in the car and wonder where we were going as we hurtled off to my new life.

The car suddenly made a turn, slowed down, and came to a stop. This was it. The Lady got out of the car and then came around to get her purse and me. As she reached for me, I felt a new gentleness that had not been there before. It felt wonderful.

As I held my breath, I looked over her shoulder as the next part of my journey unfolded. I couldn't believe my eyes! I was back at The Big White House where I had been so happy! Perhaps The Lady was just stopping by to pick something up before we left again. I was trembling as she walked up the back steps cradling me in her arms.

We entered to the barking of dogs once again. This time, I had no fear because I knew that Arthur was actually excited to see me! To most it sounded like barking and growling, but he was actually welcoming me home! "Walter! Welcome home! I can't believe my eyes! Is Sophie all right? Where is that cat?" I told him that all was well and I would try to fill him in soon.

So many of my friends were at their posts. I could see the look of awe in their eyes as I was carried past them. No bear had EVER returned after being escorted out the door with

The Big Brown One and his red cape! Here I was, returning with an amazing story to tell that would have to wait until it was safe to share. I could hear their whispers of "He's back! I can't believe it! Perhaps we will get some answers now," and "Welcome home, Walter! We missed you!"

We went through the dining room and The Giraffe nodded imperceptibly as we passed her. The look on her face could only be described as joyful. Other eyes followed me as we started up the stairs. I could faintly hear the warnings from The Love Bears and The Keeper of the Stairs as we ascended. At the top of the stairs, I searched for that one face I loved the most. The Lady stopped in the library as I frantically searched for that white bear I loved so much on our rocking chair . . . Ivy! My dearest friend wasn't anywhere! Oh no! Could it be that I would return only to find Ivy gone on a Howard Journey? My heart felt like it would break! The Lady put down a book that Sophie had given her and headed toward the hallway again. By now, I was frantic! No Ivy anywhere!

Mr. Bear and Blankie

Chapter Twenty-Four
Full Circle

"A loving friendship is when you have complete trust and faith in the other. The rest is just icing on the cake."
The Loved Bears on the Bed

Then The Lady carried me into the bedroom. As I glanced around, I could see many beloved faces that were thrilled to see my return! With a mixture of happiness and sorrow, I waved at them and asked about Ivy in a whisper. They only smiled and pointed. Following their paws' direction, I looked at the chosen bears on the bed who had been loved and now lived in that place of honor. There she was, my Ivy, sitting among those bears who had proven their worth and were beloved. I saw tears in her eyes and an outstretched paw as my own vision blurred. What had she been through to win this honored spot among the bears that were most loved?

To my wonder, The Lady looked me right in the eyes and said, "Well, Little Guy, you have certainly been loved. I do believe it is time to have you join the other bears on this bed!" I couldn't believe it! She gave me a kiss on the head and placed me right between Mr. Bear and Ivy! As she left the room, a hush fell over The Bedroom Bears. Then there was a multitude of voices asking questions, welcoming me home, congratulating me on my new status and simply squealing with delight!

I looked at Ivy and said, "I thought my heart would break as I was carried through the house and I couldn't find you anywhere! Before I tell my story, I want to hear how you ended up on the bed."

Ivy held my paw tightly and shared her story. "One night, I heard crying down the hallway coming from one of the little grand-daughters who was sleeping over for the night. All the bears were alerted and we took our position as The Lady ran down the hall to see what was going on. The youngest one, Beth, was sobbing and we could hear her cough and cough!

"The Lady took her temperature and decided Beth needed to be seen by a doctor right away! As she bundled her up with a blanket from the Reading Room, she looked around and grabbed me. 'Here, Beth,' she said, 'this is Howard and you need only to hold on to the bear and everything will be okay.'

"We ended up at the hospital," Ivy continued, "where the little girl seemed to get worse and worse. The doctors and nurses tried everything and yet she was having more trouble breathing each hour. The Lady, The Man, and her parents would not leave her side! All this time, she would not let go of me! Even when she needed X-rays or other treatments, she would cry out if someone tried to take me out of her arms. Finally, after many days and nights, it seemed that she was getting slightly better. They started to unhook some of the machines that whirred and hummed and she smiled for the first time in a week. She was going to get better!

"When she got to come home, she would not be separated from me under any circumstances. Finally, she was well enough to get up and eventually became her old self again. Although she didn't need me like before, she told The Lady, Beth's grandmother, that she loved me and wanted to make sure I was always safe and cherished. She handed me to her grandmother and asked her to watch over me. When she visited The Big White House, she would make sure her grandmother was following orders. That is how I got placed on the bed with the other loved bears! It never occurred to me that you might be on a similar Howard journey with a stranger!"

So we had both been Howards and learned about love in such different ways! What an honor!

At this point, The Colonel slowly, silently floated into the room to congratulate me. "I want to commend you, Walter, for bravery and compassion above and beyond expectations! You can now tell all of the bears what actually happens when you get the name Howard and leave with The Big Brown One and his cape . . . that amazing red bandana that tells the world he is there to bring comfort. If I had told all the other troops about Howard missions, they would never have believed me! I couldn't risk disorder in the ranks! I can now train them for their work in the field."

I knew that my story would be shared and bring warmth and relief to all of the bears at The Big White House. Before I visited with the other friends I had missed so much, I took a moment to simply hold Ivy's paw, sit with The Bed Bears, and feel so very loved.

Walter

Chapter Twenty-Five
Life is Good

"It only takes one small act of kindness to
change the world . . ."
The Lady

I told my story to The Bed Bears and it was
repeated many times up and down the stairs.
There was no more fear of being named Howard, only joy and pride followed future bears
out the door of The Big White House. When
a Howard was leaving, all of the bears would
cheer and wave! It was an honor to be chosen!
Not many friends returned, but we all knew
they had gone out to fill a person's life with
love and companionship. What could be better than that?

Ivy and I got to stay with The Bed Bears
in the place of honor, but we often chatted
with other bears in the house. The young ones
would ask for my story to be repeated over
and over while the older bears simply mar-

veled at my journey and waited their turn to be Howard.

As I think back on my time with Sophie and my return to The Big White House, I am humbled by the journey. I left a frightened bear with little faith in the future and returned knowing how it felt to be truly loved. For if we love and are loved in return, if we make someone's journey brighter or somebody's heart lighter, then we have served our purpose. I was honored to have been a Howard and now rejoice as other bears are chosen to make the world a better place.

If you ever stop by The Big White House, don't worry about the barking dogs or the ghost that floats up to greet you at the entry. Just tell them you are here to meet Walter and hear his story. I would be pleased to share my adventure with you!

Rivershore Books

www.rivershorebooks.com
blog.rivershorebooks.com
www.facebook.com/rivershore.books
www.twitter.com/rivershorebooks
Info@rivershorebooks.com